Enid Blyton

The Teddy Bear's Tail

...and other stories

D1364390

Bounty
Books

Published in 2014 by Bounty Books,
a division of Octopus Publishing Group Ltd,
Carmelite House
50 Victoria Embankment
London EC4Y 0DZ
www.octopusbooks.co.uk

An Hachette UK Company
www.hachette.co.uk
Enid Blyton ® Text copyright © 2014 Hodder & Stoughton Ltd.
Illustrations copyright © 2014 Octopus Publishing Group Ltd.
Layout copyright © 2014 Octopus Publishing Group Ltd.

Illustrated by Dorothy Hamilton.

ISBN: 978-0-75372-669-3

A CIP catalogue record for this book is available from the
British Library.

Printed and bound by CPI Group (UK) Ltd, Croydon, CR0 4YY

3 5 7 9 10 8 6 4

CONTENTS

1

The Rude Little Rabbit

There was once a little speckled rabbit called Bobtail who was very rude. He called cheeky names out after anyone he met, and he always answered back when anyone scolded him.

'Hallo, pins and needles!' he would say to Prickles the hedgehog. Prickles always got very much annoyed when anyone called him that.

'I shall tell your mother,' Prickles said.

'Tell my father and my mother, my brothers and my sisters, my grand-mothers and grandfathers, my great-grandmothers and my great-grand-fathers!' Bobtail said.

'I suppose you think you're clever,' said Prickles.

'I don't think it, I know it!' sang out Bobtail.

Then he saw the beautiful kingfisher fly down to the tree. The blue and green bird was dazzling to look at, but he hadn't much of a tail, which always made him feel a bit sad.

'Left your tail at home this morning?' asked Bobtail, popping his head out of a bush.

'If you were my child I'd spank you and put you to bed,' said the kingfisher, annoyed.

'If I were your child I'd find you a new tail and stitch it on!' said Bobtail rudely.

But one day he was rude to the wrong person! He was rude to the Spotted Goblin, who lived in the hollow oak tree.

The Spotted Goblin had once dropped a pot of red paint, and it had splashed up and spotted him with red all over. As it was magic paint, he hadn't been able to wash it off, so he had to have the spots for always.

Bobtail saw him coming along, and he pulled his whiskers and thought of a joke. He knew that measles had spots so he called out after the Goblin:

'Hallo, Measles! How are your spots?'

The Goblin turned round and glared. 'If you dare to say that again I'll put a spell on your ears!' he said.

Bobtail didn't believe him. 'Hallo, Measles, how are your spots?' he said again, and then rushed off to his hole at once.

'Kikky, rooni, billinoona!' shouted the Goblin in an angry voice. It was a spell for rabbits' ears, but Bobtail didn't know it.

The spell worked. When Bobtail got to his hole and tried to flatten his ears down over his head, as all rabbits must do when they run underground, Bobtail found that he couldn't put his ears down at all! No, they just stayed upright. It was strange.

10

He tried to force his way into the hole. His mother saw him, and spoke to him sharply. 'You've left your ears up. Put them down, silly child.'

'I can't,' said Bobtail, in dismay.

'Don't be stupid!' said his mother. 'All rabbits can put their ears down.'

But Bobtail couldn't. It wasn't a bit of good. His ears stayed straight up, and even when his mother tried to bend them down she couldn't. She only made Bobtail cry out with pain.

11

'Well, you can't come into the burrow unless you put your ears down,' said his mother. 'You'll wear them out. What have you been doing to get your ears like this?'

'I was rude to the Spotted Goblin,' said Bobtail, looking ashamed. 'I said: "Hallo, Measles, how are the spots?"'

'What! You were as rude as that!' cried his mother. 'I'm ashamed of you. You deserve to have a spell put into your ears, you really do.'

Well, poor Bobtail had a bad time after that. You see, he couldn't dash into his hole with all the other rabbits when an enemy came along. Sometimes it was a sly fox, coming to get a young rabbit for dinner. Sometimes it was a dog hunting. Other times it was a farmer with a gun.

Bobtail dashed off into the bushes, but it was easy for foxes or dogs to smell him out. He ran and ran, and they ran after him. He only managed to escape by leaping into a hollow tree and staying there quite still whilst his enemies rushed past.

'This is dreadful,' thought poor Bobtail. 'What a life I shall lead with ears like this. I never knew before how important it is for a rabbit's ears to be able to flop over.'

One day he saw the Spotted Goblin standing at the top of Steep Hill. Bobtail made his way humbly to him.

'Please, Spotted Goblin,' he said. 'I'm very sorry I was rude to you. Take the spell out of my ears. I'll never be rude to anyone again.'

The Rude Little Rabbit

'I can't take the spell out,' said the Goblin. 'There's only one way of curing those long ears of yours – and that is to throw you from the top of the hill to the bottom!'

'Oh no, oh no!' cried Bobtail, wishing he had never gone near the Goblin. But the Spotted Goblin lunged out with his foot and gave Bobtail a hard kick.

He rolled down the hill, over and over, over and over, head and back and heels and ears and tail, over and over. His ears were bent and he squealed in pain. He lost two whiskers. He hurt his foot. He bruised his bobtail – and he certainly bent his ears back till they nearly broke!

He sat up, feeling very shaky, at the bottom of the hill. He felt himself all over to see if he was still there. Two young rabbits came out to look at him.

'Do you usually come down the hill like that?' they said.

'Now don't you be cheeky!' said Bobtail, and he turned to chase them. They went down their hole – and he followed them. Half-way down he stopped in delight.

'My ears are all right again! They bent themselves down when I went into the hole. Oh good – now they are cured!'

But it was a very painful cure, for Bobtail was so stiff and bruised for days after that he could hardly lollop in and out of his hole.

'I hope you're cured of your rudeness now,' his mother said to him.

'Mother, I'm the very politest rabbit that ever was,' said Bobtail.

'What a change!' said his mother. And it certainly was!

2

Fred's Forgettery

There was once a boy who had a very bad memory. He didn't even *try* to remember anything, which made things even worse!

'Fred, you haven't got a memory, you've only got a forgettery!' his mother said to him, many times. 'Didn't I remind you three times to call at the shoemaker's for your shoes and *now* you haven't remembered!'

'Oh Mother, I quite forgot,' said Fred.

'But did you *try* to remember?' asked his mother. 'No, you didn't. Now you will have to wear your old shoes with your new suit when you go to see Granny. That really is a pity.'

One day the circus came to Fred's town. It really was a marvellous one. It

17

was Mr. Phillippino's, and there were elephants, a giraffe, monkeys, and the funniest clowns you ever saw.

Some of the children went, and they really loved it. Fred wanted to go, but as he had really been very silly that week, his mother said no.

'You forgot to take your books to school yesterday, and lost a good mark for that,' she said. 'And on Monday you forgot I had asked you to stay at school to lunch and you came home, and made a great fuss because I was out and there was no one to get you your meal. And

18

this very morning I asked you to call at the paper shop and bring me back my paper, and you didn't. No, you don't deserve a ticket for the circus. That forgettery of yours is playing all kinds of tricks this week!'

Now, on Thursday evening Fred had to go to a nearby friend's house to borrow a school book he had forgotten. As he came back with it he saw an old man hurrying to catch the post.

'The post has gone!' thought Fred. 'I saw the postman collecting the letters as I came by. The old man has missed the post.'

The man stopped by the pillar-box and looked at the post-times, as he held up the letter to the slit in the red box. Then he gave a cry of annoyance, for he saw that there was no collection until the next day. He had missed the last post.

'What a nuisance!' Fred heard him say. 'Missed the post! Now the letter won't get there till Saturday morning if I post it. I'd better deliver it myself.'

Fred's Forgettery

He stopped Fred as the boy came by. 'Do you know where Rockland School is?' he asked. 'Is it far?'

'Yes, a good way,' said Fred. 'It's my school. I go there every day. You go down there and turn to the left and . . .'

'Wait a minute, wait a minute – did you say *you* go to Rockland School?' asked the old man. 'Well, I wonder if you'd mind taking this letter with you tomorrow morning, without fail, and giving it to the headmaster?'

'Oh yes, of course,' said Fred, and he held out his hand for the note. 'I can easily do that.'

'Thanks very much,' said the man. 'Now don't forget, will you? You'll be sorry if you do!'

Fred didn't tell the old fellow what a forgettery he had! He took the note and put it into his pocket, quite meaning to give it to the headmaster the next morning.

He didn't think to himself, 'Now I *must* remember this – I will carry it home in my hand, and put it on my dressing-table so that I shall see it tomorrow morning. Then if I carry it in my hand all the way to school, I simply won't be able to help remembering to deliver it!'

No – he didn't try to remind himself at all that he had something to do for somebody else. He just put it in his pocket – and forgot ALL about it.

He didn't once think of the letter that evening. He didn't think of it the next morning. He forgot all about it when he got to school and took off his coat. There

was the letter, safe in his coat pocket, hanging up in the cloakroom, and nobody knew it was there!

Friday came and went. Saturday morning came. That was the very last day of the circus! Fred asked his mother again if he could go, but she shook her head.

'I should think not, Fred! Do you know you forgot to call in and ask how poor old Mrs. Jones was yesterday, and I reminded you six times at least. The poor old thing was very hurt because I didn't send to ask how she was.

Certainly you can't have treats if you don't even *try* to remember!'

Fred went out to play with his friends. They went to peep in between the railing round the field where the circus camp was. It did look so exciting. The boys wished and wished they could see it.

'The tickets are expensive,' said one boy. 'Usually they are half-price for children, but this circus has done so well, and been so crowded every night, that there have been no half-price tickets. I think the circus-owner must be jolly mean!'

Saturday went and Sunday came. That day the circus moved off. Some of the boys watched it. It was fun to see the elephants move away, dragging caravans behind them. The clowns no longer looked like clowns, for they were dressed in ordinary old jerseys and trousers. The horses were not so beautiful without their waving plumes. All the same, it was exciting to watch, as the big procession slowly made its way out of the field.

Fred's Forgettery

Monday morning came. All the boys went back to school again, and gathered together in the big hall for prayers and roll-call. They were about to go to their classrooms when the headmaster stood up again. He had something to say.

'One moment, boys,' he said. 'I have something to tell you. I have had a letter, this morning, from the owner of the circus that was here last week. I will read it to you.'

The boys stood still, listening. The head began to read the letter.

'Dear Mr. Kenley,

I was astonished not to see the boys of your school at the circus on Saturday evening. I had hoped that you would allow them all to come and take the front seats, as I had offered them to you free. I hope you got the invitation safely. I gave it to one of your boys on Thursday evening to deliver to you for me as I had missed the post. He promised to do this.

Yours faithfully,

"Phillippino."'

The headmaster folded up the letter and looked down from the platform at the surprised boys. They were nudging one another and whispering!

'We could have had the front seats! They're the best!'

'Who took the note? Why didn't he give it to the head?'

'What a shame! The circus has gone now and we can't see it.'

One boy stood without saying a word, his face as red as a beetroot. That boy was Fred! Of course – that old man by the letter-box was Phillippino, the owner of the circus – and he had given the invitation to Fred – and he had forgotten all about it. It must be in his pocket still!

'I've robbed all the boys of the chance of seeing the circus for nothing!' thought Fred, with horror. 'Oh, why didn't I *try* to remember?'

'Well, boys,' said the headmaster, putting the letter into his pocket, 'if Mr. Phillippino is right, one of you took the invitation from him, and forgot to deliver it. Who was it?'

Fred was frightened to say it was he who had forgotten. The boys would be so angry. He stood there, saying nothing, his face still red.

'Come, come!' said the headmaster, impatiently. 'No one is away today. It must have been one of you. It is bad enough to forget to deliver a letter, but it is a great deal worse not to be brave enough to own up to it. I've no doubt it was quite by accident that the note was not delivered to me, but please don't make matters worse by not owning up.'

Fred was terribly ashamed of himself. Was he a coward as well as a careless forgetter? Yes, he was coward – but he'd put a stop to *that!* He would own up.

He heard his own voice, rather shaky and small.

'Please, Mr. Kenley, sir, *I* got the note. I put it into my pocket, and forgot all about it. It's there still.'

There was a silence. The boys glared at Fred in anger, and then began whispering, calling the boy all kinds of hard names because he had made them miss going to the circus.

'Fetch the note,' said the Head. Fred went out and brought the letter back. The Head opened it and read it out loud.

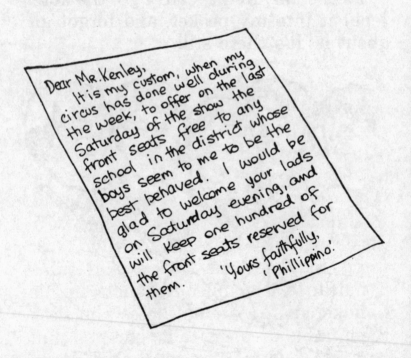

Dear Mr. Kenley,

It is my custom, when my circus has done well during the week, to offer on the last Saturday of the show the front seats free to any school in the district whose boys seem to me to be the best behaved. I would be glad to welcome your lads on Saturday evening, and will keep one hundred of the front seats reserved for them.

'Yours faithfully,
'Phillippino.'

'Well!' said the headmaster, folding up the note. 'I'm afraid Fred has spoilt the treat for you. Fred, will you kindly write an explanation and an apology to Mr. Phillippino today. Dismiss!'

Fred had a bad time that day. Every boy was disgusted, disappointed and angry.

'Can't you remember *any*thing? You're not stupid, just lazy!'

'It's all very well to forget things that only concern yourself, but when you spoil something for other people it's different!'

'Let's leave him out of games. Who wants a boy who can't even remember to deliver a note for an old man!'

It was a tremendous shock for Fred. He must get rid of his forgettery! He must remind himself to remember things in all sorts of ways, even if it was a nuisance. He must tie knots in his handkerchief, write out notes and stick them in his dressing-table glass so that he could read them in the morning and remember. He must keep saying to himself, 'What did Mother tell me today? What did Mr. Kenley ask me to do?'

'I must get back my memory and lose my forgettery,' said Fred. 'Then perhaps the boys will forget what I have done, and forgive me. It's so horrid having no friends at school.'

So he is trying hard, but it's very difficult. What's *your* memory like? I do hope it's not a forgettery like Fred's!

3

The Cat Without a Tail

In Cherry Road there were six houses side by side, and in every house there was either a dog or a cat or both.

There was Scamper the terrier, and Tiddles the tabby. There were Smut and Soot, two black cats so alike that hardly anyone knew the difference. There was Scottie the Scottie dog. There was Tinker the mongrel. He was just a mixture of a lot of dogs. And there was Ginger the cat, whose coat was the colour of marmalade.

Now one day a new cat came to the house whose garden backed on to the six houses in Cherry Road. At first the other cats, sitting on walls or fences, only just caught a peep, but they said she looked a nice little cat. They thought they would like to know her.

But the new little cat was shy and frightened. She didn't seem to want to

make friends. She vanished indoors as soon as any other cat appeared, and as for dogs, she was really scared of them.

The dogs and cats of Cherry Road talked to one another about the new cat.

'She's grey,' said Scamper the terrier.

'She's small,' said Smut and Soot.

'She's got a very tiny mew,' said Tiddles the tabby.

'Her eyes are green,' said Scottie.

'She's the only animal in that house,' said Ginger, the orange-coloured cat.

'I'd like to chase her,' said Tinker the mongrel.

35

The cats turned to stare at him, looking down their noses scornfully.

'You *would!*' they said. 'You have no manners. You are a common little mongrel.'

'Mongrels should be seen and not heard,' said the dogs. 'In fact,' said Scottie, 'I think it's a pity they should even be seen or smelt.'

'You're always horrid to me,' said poor Tinker. And so they were. He had tried to make friends with each one in turn, but they all turned their noses up at him. Smut and Soot were friends, of course. Tiddles and Scottie were firm friends too, and often slept in the same basket together. Ginger and Scamper were friends, though they did not live in the same house. Only Tinker had no friend.

The other cats and dogs thought he was a horrid, common little dog. He was a merry fellow, always wanting to play, and as sharp as could be. But none of the others would have anything to do with him at all. So poor Tinker had to

run round and round after his own tail when he wanted a game, which was fun at first, but boring after a while because he couldn't help knowing that his tail grew on the end of himself.

Now, the very next day, the little new cat jumped up on the sunny wall that divided her garden from the one at the back. All the other cats and dogs ran to speak to her – but as soon as she saw them, down she jumped and ran for the house as fast as she could.

But not before the animals had seen something very strange indeed.

'She hasn't got a tail!' said Tiddles, uncurling her beautiful grey one.

'I thought that too,' said Scamper, wagging his.

'How very peculiar!' said Smut and Soot.

'Poor, poor thing – someone must have bitten it off,' said Ginger.

'A dog must have chased her,' said Scottie. 'A dog that knew no better.'

'Yes, and that dog must be Tinker,' said Scamper at once. 'Didn't he say he would like to chase the little new cat?

38

Disgusting animal! First he chases the poor creature, then he bites off her tail! I vote we don't speak to him any more.'

'Not a word!' said Smut and Soot.

'I always did say he was a horrid, common little mongrel,' said Tiddles. 'So did we,' said Smut and Soot.

Just then Tinker ran up, wagging his tail. 'Woof,' he said. 'What do you think? The butcher's boy . . .'

Then he stared in astonishment – for all the cats and dogs put their noses into the air and walked off. Not one mew or

bark could Tinker get out of them. He was puzzled and unhappy.

'What's the matter?' he barked. 'What have I done now?'

'Don't you dare to bark to us!' yowled Tiddles. 'We don't talk to dogs who chase little new cats and bite off their tails.'

'I didn't. I didn't!' yelped Tinker. But nobody believed him.

'Fibber!' said Ginger, and hissed.

'Story-teller!' said Scamper, and wuffed. 'Go away. We don't want to have any more to do with you.'

Poor Tinker. He was very sad. He found that the cats and dogs really did mean what they said, and it wasn't a bit of good going to them and begging them to talk to him. So he kept away, and put his tail and ears down, feeling very unhappy.

One day he went to the bottom of the garden and lay down sadly, wishing his mistress would move, so that he might make a friend somewhere else. 'Though I do believe no one will ever make friends with a funny-looking dog like me,' thought Tinker. 'My ears are too long. My legs are too short. My tail is too curly. I'm an ugly dog.'

'What's the matter?' said a voice above him. 'Why do you whine like that?'

Tinker looked up. He saw the little new cat sitting on the wall. He put his head down on his paws with a grunt.

'Don't talk to me,' he said. 'You are the cause of all my trouble.'

'Why?' asked the little new cat.

41

'Because everyone says I have chased you and bitten off your tail,' said Tinker, gloomily.

'Well, you didn't,' said the little new cat, with a purr that sounded like a laugh.

'Who did?' asked Tinker.

'Nobody,' said the cat.

'Well, did you get it caught in a trap, then?' said Tinker.

'No. I never had one,' said the little new cat. 'I'm a Manx cat, and Manx cats don't have long tails. I've just got a stump of a tail. Look. We never grow long ones.'

Tinker looked. He was very surprised. 'It's not very pretty to have no tail,' he said.

'I suppose not,' said the Manx cat. 'I'm always afraid of being laughed at or jeered at. So, as soon as I see any other dog or cat coming I jump away and go into the house. But it's very lonely, being somebody different. You can never make friends.'

'I feel like that too,' said Tinker. 'You

see, I'm only a mixture dog, a mongrel dog. I'm not a terrier or a spaniel or a bulldog – I'm a kind of mixture, and the others don't like me. Now they won't speak to me because they say I chased you and bit off your tail.'

'How silly,' said the Manx cat. 'Do be friends with me. You are a bit ugly, but you've nice brown eyes and a lovely wag in your tail. My name is Shorty. What's yours?'

'Tinker,' said Tinker, joyfully. 'Come into my garden and play.'

So Shorty jumped down and soon she and Tinker were having a marvellous game of Round and Round the Raspberry Canes. They made such a noise that all the other animals came to see what it was.

'Tinker is friends with the little new cat!' said Ginger. 'I must say she looks a nice little thing, even though she's got no tail.'

'Tinker can't have bitten it off,' said Tiddles. 'If he had, she wouldn't like him.'

'I'd like to be friends with her,' said Scamper, longing to join in the game. 'Sorry, Tinker, for saying things about you!'

'Well – you can play if you want to,' said Tinker, who was very forgiving. But the Manx cat didn't want to play with anyone but Tinker. She jumped up on to the wall and fled away.

'She's a bit particular about her friends, is little Shorty!' said Tinker, with a twinkle in his brown eyes. 'I'm rather particular too. I don't think I want anyone but Shorty.'

He strolled off and the others looked after him. They badly wanted to make friends with him now that he didn't seem to want them!

And after that Tinker had a grand time! He and Shorty became fast friends – and when she wasn't there to have a game, he could play with any of the others.

'And be careful I don't bite off your tails!' he would bark to them. 'Woooof! I'm after you!'

4

Eggs and Marbles

Jack and Jim were twins and they did everything together. They went to school together, played Red Indians together, ran races together, played marbles, and went bird-nesting with one another.

Their mother didn't mind anything they did, except that she hated them to take the eggs out of the birds' nests.

'It makes the birds so sad,' she said. 'It is so unkind of you, Jack and Jim. You don't want the eggs. You don't collect them. You just find the nest, see the eggs, and take them. It isn't fair of you. Let the birds have them – they don't belong to you, they belong to the birds.'

But Jack and Jim went on taking the eggs just the same. Their mother found the bright, blue eggs belonging to the hedge-sparrow on the mantelpiece of the boys' bedroom. She was sad, because she loved the neat little brown hedge-sparrows that came about the garden in winter.

'If you keep taking the eggs, we shall soon have no birds,' she said. 'Now listen – I will give you some beautiful glass marbles, if you will promise me not to take any more eggs.'

The boys loved playing marbles. They promised at once that they would take no more eggs. Their mother took them to a toy shop and bought them eight of the loveliest marbles you can imagine. They were very large, made of glass, and inside the glass were patterns of blue, red and yellow, curving like snakes. Jack and Jim were really delighted.

'Oh, Mother! Aren't they simply beautiful!' said Jack. 'The other children *will* think we are lucky to have these! They will be our very best marbles.'

The two boys were very proud indeed of the wonderful marbles. They showed them to the other children, who tried to make the twins exchange them for sweets, chocolates or toys – but Jack and Jim wouldn't.

'No,' said Jack. 'They are the best marbles in the world. We shall never part with them. We shall keep them till

we are grown up, and even then we won't give them away.'

The twins kept their word to their mother for a while, and did not take a single egg. Then, coming home from school one day, Jack saw a robin fly up from the ditch nearby.

'I bet there's a nest there,' he said, and he began to look. Sure enough, there was a nest, made of moss and dead leaves. In the nest were three pretty red-brown eggs.

'Robins' eggs,' said Jack. 'Let's take them.'

'We said we wouldn't,' said Jim. 'Look out – there's the robin come back. Hallo – it's angry!'

The little hen robin was indeed angry. The twins had robbed her first nest of eggs, and her second one as well. Now she had laid three more eggs in this nest, and she wanted to hatch them, and have the joy of seeing tiny nestlings cuddled in the cosy nest.

She flew right into Jack's face, and then flapped round Jim's head. The boys laughed. 'Silly little thing! As if *you* could stop us taking your eggs! We'll take them just to spite you.'

The two boys took the three little warm eggs from the nest. The robin was broken-hearted. She flew angrily round their heads, making such a noise that two big jackdaws, flying overhead, came down to see what the matter was.

They found the little robin sitting on the edge of her nest. Her heart filled with sadness. Her third batch of eggs was gone. It wasn't any good laying any more. She would have no little ones

to feed and love that summer.

The jackdaws listened to all she sang to them. 'It's time we did something to stop those boys from robbing our nests,' said the first jackdaw. 'Do boys have eggs of their own? Shall we go and steal *their* eggs?'

The robin didn't know anything about boys, except that they stole eggs from her nest and from the nests of other birds. 'I wish you *would* steal their

51

eggs, if they have any,' she sang, in her creamy voice. 'I wish you would!'

The jackdaws flew off. They saw the house the boys went into. They flew down to the roof. Then they heard the voices of the boys in the bedroom below.

'We'd better hide these robin eggs; Mother would be very upset if she saw them. After all, we did promise we wouldn't take any more.'

The jackdaws waited until they could no longer hear voices, and then they flew down to the window-sill of the bedroom, and walked about the floor, looking for any eggs that might belong to the boys.

'Look!' said the first jackdaw, suddenly. 'Eggs! Large, round eggs, all bright and shining.'

The other jackdaw looked. In a box, arranged on cotton wool, were the eight beautiful glass marbles belonging to the boys. The big birds had no idea they were playthings. To them they seemed like big round eggs.

'These are the eggs belonging to the

Eggs and Marbles

two boys,' clacked the first jackdaw.
'See the nest of wool they are in! We will
take all the eggs away. Then they will
not hatch and the boys will know what
it is to feel unhappy.'

So, one by one, the jackdaws carried
away the big glass marbles. They took
them to their own enormous nest of
sticks, high up in the church tower.
There they put the eight wonderful
marbles.

The twins came upstairs just as the
jackdaws flew out of the window with
the last two marbles in their beaks.
They gave a scream.

'Our marbles! Mother, Mother, quick!
The jackdaws have taken our marbles.
They're all gone! Mother, Mother!'

Their mother came running in. She
looked at the empty box.

'Poor Jack – poor Jim!' she said. 'You
know, jackdaws love bright, shining
things. They must have come along and
seen your marbles, and taken them off.
They once took a silver thimble of mine.'

'No, Mother, no, they didn't take our

marbles because they like shiny things,' sobbed Jack, so upset that he couldn't help owning up to his mother. 'We broke our promise to you – we took some robin eggs – there they are, look, in this drawer – and I'm sure the jackdaws have come along and taken our marbles to punish us! We saw two flying overhead when we stole the robin eggs.'

Mother looked shocked and sad. 'To take eggs is horrid – but to break your

word to me when I trusted you is dreadful,' she said. 'To think that my own little boys should do that, when they love me and I love them!'

She didn't say any more. She went downstairs by herself. The boys were dreadfully upset, because they really did love their mother. They rushed after her to comfort her.

'We'll never do it again!'

'You can trust us, you can really!'

'We're awfully sorry. Forgive us and give us another chance, Mother. Don't look like that!'

'Of course I'll forgive you and give you another chance,' said their mother. 'But I'm afraid you've lost your marbles.'

They had. They are in the nest of the jackdaws, high up in the church tower – but they haven't hatched yet!

5

Sally's Stitch

Sally was a little girl who was always laughing, so you can guess she was rather nice. I do like people who laugh, don't you? Well, you would have liked Sally very much. Everybody did.

One day she went for a walk across the fields. She went quietly, for the grass was thick and soft. And quite suddenly she came across five or six pixies playing the most surprising games. Sally knew they were pixies because she had seen pictures of them in books, just as you have. She was simply delighted. She sat down behind a bush and watched.

'I can stand on my head on the gate-post!' cried a small pixie – and he did. It was really funny to see him.

'I can curl myself up into a ball and roll along!' cried another. And he curled himself up, arms and legs and all, and began to roll over and over just like a ball. All the pixies laughed to see him.

'Can you bounce yourself, can you bounce yourself?' squealed a pixie nearby. 'Oh, do try!'

'Of course I can!' cried the ball-pixie, and he threw himself up into the air. 'Look out – I'm going to bounce!'

And he bounced. Goodness, how he bounced! Just as if he were a big rubber ball. Up into the air he went, and down he came again. He bounced on to a prickly thistle, gave a loud yell, and bounced high again.

Sally began to laugh. She couldn't help it. She laughed till the tears came into her eyes. Then she got a stitch in her side from laughing, and that made her feel very uncomfortable. 'Oh dear,' she said, 'oh dear!' And she put her hand against her side to try and ease the stitch there. You know how funny you feel when you get a stitch in your

side from running or laughing, don't you?

The pixies heard Sally's laughter. It was a nice sound. They ran round the

bush to see who was there. And they found Sally, laughing away, with her hand pressed to her side.

'What's the matter?' they cried anxiously. 'Why do you hold yourself there? Are you hurt?'

'Oh, I've got such a big stitch in my side!' said Sally. 'I can't breathe properly. I can't walk with it, either.'

'Poor little girl!' cried a big pixie. 'Who put the stitch there? Did you sew it there yourself? Was the needle sharp?'

'Of course not,' said Sally, beginning to giggle again. 'Don't be so silly.'

'Poor child!' said the pixies, looking at Sally out of their funny green eyes. 'She's got a stitch in her side. Somebody has stitched her up so that she can't walk properly. Poor child.'

'Oh, don't make me laugh again or my stitch will get worse!' cried Sally. 'Oh dear – it's the worst stitch I've ever

had. But really, you did look so funny when you bounced on that thistle, pixie. Oh my – I shall start laughing again if I'm not careful!'

She tried to walk a few steps, but she couldn't because of the stitch in her side. The pixies felt really sorry for her. They talked among themselves.

'Let's call Dame Snippit. She can take out the stitch. The poor girl will never get home. What a shame that somebody has stitched her up like that.'

'Dame Snippit! Dame Snippit!' called a pixie, loudly. 'Are you anywhere about? You're wanted.'

To Sally's enormous surprise, a neat little door opened in a nearby oak tree and out stepped a funny, plump old dame, with her hair in ringlets, and her waist all hung with scissors and tape-measures.

'What's the matter?' she asked.

'This poor child has got a stitch in her side, so she can't walk,' explained a pixie. 'Can you take out the stitch?'

'I could snip it,' said Dame Snippit,

taking up her largest pair of scissors.
'That's the quickest way of taking out a
stitch, you know.'

'Oh, I don't want it snipped,' said Sally,
in alarm. 'It's not that kind of stitch,
really it isn't.'

'Well, what sort of a stitch is it then,
my dear?' asked Dame Snippit, in
surprise.

'Well – it's a laughing-stitch,' said
Sally.

'Never heard of one,' said Dame
Snippit. 'Come, come – let me snip it for
you, then you can walk. You shouldn't
let people put a stitch in your side like
that. Very silly of you.'

'I didn't, I didn't,' said Sally, and she
tried to run away. But the stitch in her
side caught her and she had to stop. She
saw Dame Snippit take up her scissors
again.

Then Sally remembered that her
mother had always said she could get rid
of a stitch in her side by bending over
and touching her toes with her fingers.

'I'd better try that before Dame

Snippit does anything stupid!' thought the little girl. So she bent herself right over and touched her toes. When she stood up straight again, lo and behold! her stitch was quite gone! Hurray!

'The stitch is gone!' she cried. 'It's all right, pixies, it's all right, Dame Snippit. The stitch is gone.'

'I suppose you broke it when you bent over,' said Dame Snippit, in astonishment. 'Well, well – don't you go having stitches inside you any more. Most uncomfortable, I call it.'

Sally said good-bye and ran home. On the way she remembered again how the pixie had bounced himself on the prickly thistle, and she stopped and began to laugh.

And she got another stitch in her side! But she didn't say a word about it. No – she wasn't going to have Dame Snippit trying to snip the stitch with her big scissors!

Do you ever get a stitch? Well, try Sally's way of curing it, and see if it goes!

6

What an Alarm

In the village of Tickle there lived a most dishonest little pixie. His name was Light-Fingers, and it was really astonishing the amount of things he took from other people without being seen.

He would take an apple from outside Dame Cherry's shop. He would take a biscuit from the tin in Mrs. Soap's store. He would pick flowers from old Dame Lucy's garden when she was out, and steal the pears from the big tree in Farmer Corn's orchard. And although everyone felt quite certain that it was Light-Fingers who was the thief, nobody ever managed to see him. He really was very clever.

'If only we could think of some way to

catch him,' said Farmer Corn.

'I don't like accusing anyone of stealing unless I actually see them doing wrong with my own eyes,' said Dame Lucy.

'Quite right,' said Dame Cherry. 'We must never accuse anyone unless we can prove ourselves to be right. But dear me, how are we to prove ourselves right about naughty little Light-Fingers?'

Tick-Tock, the watch-maker, came up at that moment. He was a little bent old fellow with eyes as bright as a bird's.

'Hello, Tick-Tock,' said Farmer Corn. 'Now just you use your brains and help us. We want to catch Light-Fingers and punish him for stealing. But we don't know how to catch him, because he's so clever. Can you think of a way?'

'Yes,' said Tick-Tock, after a moment. 'I think I can. Light-Fingers comes by my shop every day on his way to and from the market. I'll put a clock on my window-sill and a notice on my door that says 'GONE OUT.' And if Light-Fingers doesn't take that clock I'll eat my best Sunday hat!'

'But if we hide behind a bush to watch, he's sure to know,' said Farmer Corn. 'He's so very, very smart. He wouldn't take it unless he felt quite certain he wouldn't be seen and wouldn't be found out either.'

'Now listen,' said Tick-Tock, with a smile. 'That clock is going to be an *alarm*-clock – *you* know, the kind that goes off and rings a bell very loudly at a certain time. Well, I shall set the alarm for twelve o'clock, and it will go off then, just when Light-Fingers is marketing. That will give him a shock – especially when I come up and demand my clock!'

'Now that *is* a good idea!' said everyone, pleased. 'We won't be any-

where about at all when Light Fingers takes the clock; but we'll ALL be in the market at twelve o'clock!'

So the next morning, when Light-Fingers passed by Tick-Tock's little shop, his sharp eyes saw a very fine green clock sitting by itself on the shop window-sill. Light-Fingers was surprised. Then he saw the notice on the door, 'GONE OUT', and his sharp eyes gleamed. He took a quick look round.

'There's nobody about at all,' he thought to himself. 'Not a soul! This *is* a

71

bit of luck! And I've got my old suit on, too, with its big pockets! Hurrah! I can put the clock in nicely, and nobody will guess it is there, for I'll put my big red handkerchief over it.'

So in a flash the clock was in his pocket, with his red hanky draped over it. Then off to the market went Light-Fingers, whistling merrily. He thought he would be able to sell the clock for a lot of money when he went visiting in the next town.

The market seemed very full that morning. Light-Fingers was quite surprised. People seemed to be whispering together, and nudging one another. He wondered what it was all about. But nobody told him. Nobody whispered to him that an alarm-clock was going off at twelve o'clock that morning, and that he, Light-Fingers, was going to get a terrible shock!

At eleven o'clock the town crier went round the market, ringing his bell and shouting loudly:

'Lost or stolen! A beautiful green clock

from Tick-Tock's window-sill! Lost or stolen! A beautiful green clock from Tick-Tock's window-sill! Please bring to me at once if you have it!'

'I haven't seen it!' said Dame Lucy, and she turned to Light-Fingers. 'Have you?'

'Dear me, no,' said naughty Light-Fingers, untruthfully. 'If I *had* seen it, I would have taken it back to poor Tick-Tock at once.'

'I'm afraid someone must have stolen it,' said Tick-Tock, sadly. 'Light-Fingers, what do you think we ought to do to the thief, if we catch him?'

'Well, if anyone was horrid enough to steal your clock, they ought to be very well punished indeed,' said Light-Fingers. 'I think the thief ought to get one hard spank from everyone in the village. If that didn't cure him, then what about taking him to the Bad-Tempered Wizard. I'm sure *he* would cure anyone in no time!'

'Good idea!' cried everyone. 'A very good idea. We agree with you, Light-Fingers.'

Now, as twelve o'clock drew nearer, everyone pressed close to Light-Fingers, eager to hear the alarm clock go off. Light-Fingers couldn't imagine why the crowds semed to be everywhere around him. He couldn't seem to get away from

What an Alarm

them.

Then the market-clock struck twelve – and almost immediately afterwards the alarm clock went off loudly. My goodness, the noise it made! It had the loudest alarm of any clock in Tick-Tock's shop, and it made Light-Fingers almost jump out of his skin!

'R-r-r-r-r-ring! R-r-r-r-ring! R-r-r-r-ring!'

The alarm clock went off with a terrific noise. Everyone giggled. Light-Fingers jumped high into the air and clapped his hand to his pocket. Goodness! What could be happening?

'R-r-r-r-ring! R-r-r-r-ring!'

'What's that ringing? Where does the noise come from?' yelled Light-Fingers.

'It comes from your pocket,' said Tick-Tock, with such a stern look on his face that Light-Fingers suddenly felt frightened. 'WHAT have you got in your pocket?'

'N-n-n-n-nothing – except my red hanky,' stammered Light Fingers.

'Hankies don't ring like that,' said Tick-Tock.

'R-r-r-r-r-ring! R-r-r-r-ring!' went the alarm clock gaily. It seemed as if it would never stop!

'If you have nothing but your hanky in your pocket, let me see what it is that is ringing,' said Tick-Tock. 'Have you a magic ringing spell?'

'No,' said Light-Fingers. 'And, anyway, I don't want you looking into my pockets. That's a nasty thing to do.'

But before he could stop Tick-Tock, the watch-maker had put his small hand deep into Light-Fingers' pocket –

and pulled out – his alarm clock, still gaily ringing for all it was worth.

'HO!' said Tick-Tock, in a terrible stern voice. 'HO! So that is where my beautiful green alarm clock went – into your pocket where many other things have gone, I've no doubt. Light-Fingers, you are a little thief, a nasty horrid little thief. I am glad you said what the punishment for a little thief should be. Let me see – what was it?'

Light-Fingers began to tremble. 'I-I-dd-don't remember,' he stammered.

But everyone else remembered, of course. 'Light-Fingers said one hard spank from everyone in the village!' a score of voices called out gleefully. Most of the people there had had things taken from them at sometime or other by Light-Fingers, so they were pleased to think they could give him one hard spank each. That would teach the bad pixie not to steal!

And so Light-Fingers got the punishment he himself suggested, and dear me, he didn't like it at all, especially when it was Farmer Corn's turn, because his hand was simply enormous and dreadfully hard.

Tick-Tock took his clock back home, and everyone giggled when they thought of the trick the clock had played on Light-Fingers.

'And remember, pixie, just remember what you said should happen to a thief who wasn't cured by spanks,' said the watchmaker solemnly. 'You said he had better be sent to the Bad-Tempered Wizard. So BE CAREFUL!'

Light-Fingers is careful. He has been quite honest for a long time now, so perhaps he really is cured.

7

Linda's Little House

On her birthday Linda had an exciting present. She undid the paper, and unwrapped a box. On the front of the box was a picture of a pretty little house, with a green roof, some windows, a green front door, and two red chimneys.

'Oh!' said Linda. 'What a darling house!'

She took off the box-lid – and there, inside, were red bricks, green tiles for the roof, little glass windows, a small green front door and two red chimneys.

'You see, it's for you to build,' said Mummy. 'If you look well at the picture, and copy it, you will see exactly how to build that pretty little house.'

She built the walls. She slipped the windows into the spaces she had left in

the walls. She put on the green tiled roof very carefully. She slid the chimneys into the holes left for them. And last of all she put in the little front door, which could be hung on a small hinge and opened and shut properly. It even had a tiny knocker on it, which made the smallest rat-tat-tat you ever heard.

'Look, Mummy!' said Linda. 'Isn't it lovely? Now I know how to build a house! Would you like to see me do it all over again?'

'Yes, I would,' said Mummy. So Linda

knocked the tiny house down, and began to build it all over again. She knocked it down and built it six times that day. The toys watched her every time, and thought she was very clever.

That night she left the little house standing by the toy cupboard when she went to bed. The panda opened the door, bent himself down low and walked in. The teddy bear was too fat to get inside. The clockwork mouse ran in, and the small dolls from the doll's house. They all thought it was the nicest house they had ever seen.

'Isn't Linda clever to build it up like that,' said the panda. 'She's so quick, too. Really it doesn't take her ten minutes to do it!'

Linda often played with the little house. Then someone gave her a paint-box and she forgot about the house for a time, and painted pictures instead.

Now one night, when the toys were playing in the nursery, there came a knocking at the window.

'That's Dance-About the Pixie!' cried the bear and ran to open the window. It *was* Dance-About – but a very sad pixie she was. She cried so many tears on the window-sill that it looked as if it had been raining there.

'Whatever's the matter?' asked the bear.

'Oh, toys – you know my dear little house in the woods?' said Dance-About. 'The one made out of that big toadstool? Well, it's gone. A horrid boy came along this afternoon and kicked it to bits. It's a good thing I wasn't there, or I'd have been kicked to bits too. Now I've got no

house at all. There aren't any more toadstools growing. It's cold without a house – so I've come to ask you what I ought to do.'

The panda looked round at the little house Linda so often built. It was standing by the toy cupboard. 'What about Linda's house?' he said. 'I shouldn't think it would matter if you had that. It is a lovely little house, just big enough for you, Dance-About.'

'So it is,' said the pixie, dancing in at the front door, and out again. 'But how

can I take the house to the woods?'

'It knocks down, and it's quite easy to build up again,' said the bear. 'Look – this is how you knock it down.'

He knocked it all down, then the toys neatly put the bricks, the tiles, the chimneys and everything into the box, and popped on the lid. The panda and the bear between them carried the box to the woods, and Dance-About showed them where she wanted her house built.

But it wasn't so easy to build as the bear had thought. It was true he had

often watched Linda building it, but that wasn't the same as building it himself. He put the chimney where the window ought to be and didn't leave any room for the door. It was a dreadful muddle.

'We'd better go and ask Linda to come and help,' said the panda at last. 'Oh, dear - I hope she won't mind us borrowing the house like this. Bear, go and fetch her, will you?'

So, much to her surprise, Linda was awakened by the bear, who told her what they wanted. She got out of bed at once, excited.

'It was rather naughty of you, bear, to carry my house off like that without even asking me,' she said, as she put on her dressing-gown and slippers. 'Of course, I'll come – and I'll build the house and let Dance-About have it. Fancy seeing a pixie in the middle of the night like this!'

The bear took her to the place in the woods where the pixie was. All the other toys were there, too, standing round the heap of bricks and tiles on the grass.

Linda began to build the house. The moon shone down and gave her enough light to see by. In ten minutes the house was finished. There it stood in the moonlight, with its red chimneys, shining windows and little front door. It looked so real.

'Oh, thank you!' said Dance-About, skipping in at the door. 'It's beautiful. Just the right size, too. I'll get some curtains for the windows tomorrow, and buy some furniture. And I'll give a tea-

party when the house is ready to live in. You'll come, won't you, Linda?'

'Of course !' said Linda, joyfully, and off she went back to bed. She could hardly believe it was all true next day when she woke up! But the box was gone, and she was almost sure the bear gave her a smile when she looked at him.

And today she found a note tucked under the bear's fat arm. It says:

91

'Dear Linda,

My tea-party is at four o'clock to-day. Do come. Tippy-toppy tarts with cream, and Squishy Buns with honey.

Love from Dance-About.'

Linda's going, of course, and she's going to tell me what the Tippy-toppy tarts are, and the Squishy Buns. I hope she brings a few back with her, don't you!

8

The Old Black Horse

There was once an old black horse who lived by himself in Long Meadow. He was past work and he spent his days pulling at the juicy grass, and remembering his old friends and the good times they had had together.

He was lonely. His friends were far away, still at work for one farmer or another. There were sheep in the next field, but the old horse thought them stupid creatures. There were rabbits in his own field, but they always ran off as soon as they heard his heavy hoofs.

'I wouldn't mind a dog to talk to sometimes,' thought the old horse. 'I've known some friendly dogs in my time – clever dogs too. But the farmer's two dogs are surly creatures, and never

The Old Black Horse

come near me.'

At the cottage down the road lived a boy. He was big for his age, and stronger than the other lads. The old horse sometimes saw him passing by the gate, but he always kept out of the way. He didn't want to make friends with that boy!

Tom didn't make friends with anything or anyone! He had quickly found out that he was bigger and stronger than most children of his age, and so he had always got his own way by pushing

94

the others down, or hitting them hard. The other boys and girls were afraid of him, and Tom soon knew that. He liked them to be afraid of him. He liked them to run away when he came along. It made him feel grand and strong and important. He wasn't nice to animals either. He wanted them to be afraid of him too!

And they were. The old horse galloped off to the other end of the field when Tom came by. He knew quite well that Tom could throw stones very hard. It was better to be out of the boy's way! All the cats and dogs ran off when Tom came by, too. He could pull a cat's tail hard, and twist a dog's collar till the poor creature almost choked.

One day the old horse saw, to his great surprise, that Tom had a dog of his own! It was a big, clumsy puppy, with wide brown eyes and a tail that wagged gaily. Someone had given it to the boy, and Tom meant to make it the most obedient dog in the world.

'I've no use for animals who won't do

what they are told!' he said to the other boys. 'My dog is going to be my slave. When I say "Come" it will come, and when I say, "Go" it will go. When I say "Lie down" it will lie down at once.'

That was exactly like Tom. He wasn't going to make a loving friend of his dog – he was going to make it a poor frightened little slave. And he began at once.

The puppy was put on a short lead. He was made to walk close by Tom's legs, almost choking. He was hit when he did

not understand an order from Tom. He was scolded the whole time, and never praised or loved.

He soon lost the wag out of his tail, and his ears drooped. He began to be afraid of Tom. He was a dear, playful puppy, but as soon as Tom came near he crouched down on the ground and put his tail between his legs.

Tom used to give the puppy his lessons in the lane by the field where the old horse lived. The horse watched through a gap in the hedge. He liked dogs and he thought the puppy looked a jolly fellow. He felt very sorry for him.

The puppy soon learnt to do what he was told, because he knew that if he didn't he would be struck hard with a stick, or have his collar pulled at so hard that it hurt him. He was taught all sorts of things, but he did them out of fear, not out of love.

One day Tom took the puppy down the lane. He met Harry, Len and Mollie.

'Hallo,' he said. 'See my pup? Like to watch him do some tricks?'

The other children stood and watched. The puppy was told what he was to do.

'Now I'm going to throw my stick into this pond, and you are to fetch it,' said Tom.

The puppy listened. He looked at the pond. There were ducks on it and he didn't like ducks. They flapped big wings at him. Splash! Tom's stick went into the pond, and he shouted to the puppy.

'Fetch it! Fetch it!'

But the puppy wouldn't. He crouched down on the ground and shivered. The other children laughed. Tom was very angry.

'What! You won't obey me, you tiresome little thing!' he yelled. 'You shall have a beating.'

He struck the puppy with a stick and the dog howled in pain.

'Don't,' said Mollie. 'You're cruel.'

'Stop,' said Harry. 'He's only a pup.'

'I'll beat you too, if you give me orders about my own dog!' said Tom, angrily. The puppy howled again.

The old horse had been watching. He was afraid of Tom, too – but he couldn't bear to hear the dog whining so pitifully. He suddenly jumped over the hedge, and landed near the children with a crash. They all jumped, and the puppy fled behind a bush in fear.

The horse cantered up to Tom. He put his big head behind the boy's back and caught hold of his belt with his teeth. Tom felt himself suddenly jerked off his feet. Holding him tightly, though the boy was struggling hard, the old horse

99

The Old Black Horse

trotted a little way down the lane to where a big holly bush stood. The horse knew how prickly it was, for he had pricked his nose on it many times. With a jerk of his strong head he threw the boy straight into the middle of the bush!

'Ow-yow-ow!' yelled Tom, as the prickles stuck into him. 'Ow-yow-ow! You horrid thing! Get me out, Harry, quick!'

But Harry didn't. He laughed. So did the others. 'It serves you right,' said Harry. 'I'm not a bit sorry for you, Tom. You are always using your strength to hurt others weaker or smaller than yourself – and now someone stronger than you is using his strength to punish *you*. Ha, ha!'

Tom wriggled out of the bush, yelling with pain and anger. He fell to the ground, jumped up, and rushed at Harry to hit him. But the old horse stepped in again, caught hold of Tom, and this time swung him right over and into the duck-pond. There was a frightened scurrying of ducks – and

splash! Tom was in the muddy water. He came up gasping and spluttering, to see the other children screaming with laughter.

'Good old horse! It serves you right, Tom!'

The farmer came up, grinning, as Tom waded out of the pond, wet and muddy. He laid his hand on the old horse's neck.

'The old horse has done what I've longed to do many a time, my lad!' he said. 'Let it be a lesson to you. You're a bully – and my old horse has bullied you, so that you know now what it's like. Not very pleasant, is it? I've watched you bullying that pup of yours – and the other children, too. You go home and get dry – and make up your mind in the future that you will be a friend to others, and not an enemy.'

Tom went off, crying. The children ran home. The farmer put the horse back into the field, giving him a pat on his long nose. The puppy squeezed through a gap in the hedge and ran to the old horse's shaggy feet.

'Thank you,' he wuffed. 'You saved me from a beating. Perhaps Tom will be nicer now.'

'Maybe,' neighed the old horse. 'And maybe not. But you just come and tell me when he's not, and I'll deal with him again. We'll be friends, you and I.'

'We will!' yelped the puppy in delight, and galloped round and about the old horse. 'Come on – let's have a race. I like you. You're the nicest horse I've ever met.'

And now the two are great friends, and the old horse isn't lonely any more. Tom knows quite well that his puppy tells the old horse everything, and he is very careful to be kind to him instead of cruel. He doesn't want to be thrown into the pond again! It was a good thing for everyone that the old horse was sensible enough that summer's day to put matters right himself, wasn't it!

9

The Teddy Bear's Tail

The teddy bear was really tiresome. He was such a grumbler, and every day he seemed to find something new to complain about.

'I wish I could bounce,' he said, when he saw how well the ball could bounce. 'I do wish I could. I would bounce right up to the mantelpiece then, and see if I could take a sweet out of the tin there.'

Then another time he said: 'I do wish I had a key. The train has a key, and the clockwork mouse, and so has the clown. But I haven't. It isn't fair.'

When he saw the dolls sitting in a row, all beautifully dressed, he had another fine grumble.

'Look at those dolls!' he said. 'All with hats and coats and dresses and shoes!

And I haven't any clothes at all. Not even a ribbon round my neck. It isn't fair. I've only got my skin.'

'You've got a nice *furry* skin,' said the pink cat. 'Don't grumble so.'

Then the teddy found something else to grumble about. He looked behind himself for the first time and saw that he hadn't got a tail! He stared in surprise.

'Where's my tail?' he said.

'You never had one,' said the black dog.

'Why not?' asked the bear. 'I'm an animal, aren't I? Then why haven't I a tail?'

'How should I know?' said the toy dog. He wagged his own black tail, looking pleased with it.

'I've got a tail too,' squeaked the clockwork mouse.

'So have I,' said the pink cat, and she swung it round to show the bear.

'Mine's the longest,' said the toy monkey, and flapped it in the bear's face.

'Don't,' said the bear, crossly. 'Oh, I do think it's terribly unfair. *Why* haven't I got a tail? Have I lost it?'

'I told you. You never had one,' said the dog, and he gave a giggle.

Well, after that the bear was dreadfully tiresome. He went on and on grumbling because he hadn't got a tail. At last the panda could bear it no longer.

One night, when the bear had gone out on to the landing outside the nursery door, he spoke to the toys. 'For goodness' sake, let's give the bear some sort of tail. I shall go mad if I hear him wail because he's no tail.'

'Why does the teddy bear wail? Because he hasn't a tail,' said the pink cat at once, feeling clever. 'That rhymes.'

'Be quiet,' said the panda, wishing he had made up the rhyme himself. 'Now – who will give the bear his tail? Clockwork mouse, will you?'

'No,' said the mouse. 'I want mine.'

'Will you, black dog?' asked the panda. 'You've had yours for ages.'

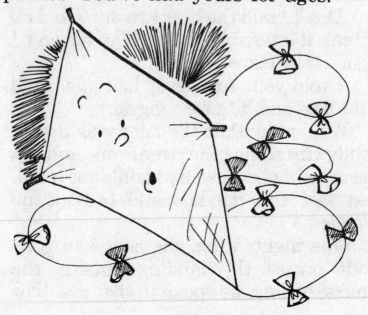

'And I want it for ages more,' said the dog. 'I keep my wag in it.'

Nobody would give up their tail. It was very annoying. But at last the old kite in the toy cupboard spoke in his funny, windy voice.

'He can have *my* tail. I'm broken now. I can't fly any more, and as I only use my tail when I fly, it's no use to me now.'

'Well – it's rather a funny tail,' said the panda doubtfully. 'I don't know if it will suit a bear.'

'Don't ask him if it will suit him,' said the kite. 'Just give it to him. Tie it on him when he's asleep. He's always grumbling because he hasn't got one, and tell him to stop grumbling.'

The toys giggled. They thought they would do that. It amused them to think of the teddy bear running about the nursery with an enormously long tail made of paper twists tied on a string! That was what the kite's tail was made of!

So, the next time the bear sat in a

corner of the toy cupboard to go to sleep, the panda snipped of the kite's tail, and neatly tied it on to the back of the teddy bear. He did it so gently that the bear didn't know it. He just lay there, fast asleep.

He woke up very soon, and stood up. He thought he would go and have a run round the nursery with the clockwork mouse, who was busy running all round the hearth-rug. The panda had wound him up, and he was having a fine time.

So the bear stepped out of the toy cupboard and began to run to the mouse. Rustle-rustle-rustle went something behind him, and he jumped in fright. He turned round quickly and saw, to his horror, that he had a long, long tail unwinding itself over the carpet.

'What is it?' he yelled.

'Your new tail,' said the panda, with a grin. 'You are always grumbling because you haven't got one, and we were so tired of hearing you – so the kite has given you his tail to wear.'

'I don't like it,' said the bear. 'Take it off!'

'What! After we have gone to all the trouble of putting it on you for a lovely surprise!' cried the pink cat. 'Ungrateful creature! Certainly we shan't take it off!'

The bear hated his new tail. For one thing it made such a rustly noise behind him. For another thing, it was so very long, and kept getting caught round table-legs and things like that, so that the bear spent half his time untangling it. Sometimes it tangled itself round his legs and made him fall over. He got very, very angry with it.

And then one day Donald, the little boy in whose nursery the toys lived, picked up his teddy, and was most astonished to see the long, long tail tied to him. He took it off at once.

'You've got all tangled up with the kite's tail!' he said. 'There – now you're all right.'

The bear was delighted. How lovely it was to run about the nursery at night again without having a horrid long tail rustling behind him and getting caught round everything. The toys looked at one another and smiled.

'Poor bear – sorry you've lost your tail,' said the panda. 'We'll get you another. A tale out of a book, perhaps.'

'I don't want a tail,' said the bear.

'Well, be careful you don't grumble again because you haven't something that other people have got,' said the panda. 'If you grumble because you've no whiskers we'll give you enormous

ones made of the hairs from the mane of the rocking horse!'

'And if you grumble because you've no key, we'll make a hole and fit the key of the clock there,' giggled the pink cat. 'Then you'll say tick-tock whenever we wind you up.'

'And if you grumble because you haven't any clothes to wear, we will dress you up like a baby doll and see how funny you look,' laughed the curly-haired doll.

'I shan't grumble any more,' said the bear, in rather a small voice. And he didn't. He was quite a nice bear after that - but there was one toy he would never, never speak to, and that was the old kite in the cupboard.

But you may be sure the kite didn't mind that!

10

The Cheeky Boy

There was once a little boy who loved to be cheeky. He spoke rudely to his mother and father, and he was cheeky even to his teacher.

He thought it was clever! It made him feel rather grand to say rude things. The other children stared at him when he said, 'Shan't!' or 'Won't,' and when he put his tongue out behind his mother's back, he felt quite a hero. The other children laughed at him sometimes, but they thought he was rather horrid, all the same.

He thought it was funny to interrupt the grown-ups when they were talking. He kept pulling his mother's arm, and pretending to want something when she was speaking to her friends. He

answered cheekily when they asked him polite questions.

'How are you, Timothy?' they would say. 'Do you like school?'

'No, I hate it,' Timothy would answer, which was not at all true. But he thought it was clever to say cheeky things like that. He would contradict people too, and that made his mother cross.

'It's very warm today,' she would say. And Timothy would answer at once: 'It isn't. It's cold as ice!'

'I wish you wouldn't be so cheeky,' his mother would sigh. 'It's so unpleasant.'

Of course, what he wanted was a good spanking, but nobody gave him that, which was great pity, because in the end he got a much bigger punishment.

It all happened one night. Timmy woke up suddenly, and heard the clock strike twelve. And at that very moment he saw what looked like a brownie in his bedroom. It was most astonishing. The boy sat up at once.

'Hallo,' said the brownie. 'I've lost my way, somehow. Is this your bedroom?'

'Oh no, it's the kitchen!' said Timothy, in his usual cheeky manner. 'Who are you?'

'I'm a brownie,' said the little fellow.

'Fibber!' said Timothy. 'There aren't any brownies, or fairies, or elves. I know that. Now you just hop off, funny-face!'

The brownie stared at him sternly. 'Have you no manners, boy?' he asked.

'Plenty,' said Timmy. 'Do you want to buy some?'

'Don't be cheeky,' said the brownie, in

disgust.

'Would you rather I was nosey?' said Timothy, in his cheekiest voice.

'My word – you must be Timothy, the cheeky boy!' said the brownie, suddenly. 'I've heard people talk about you, and say what a pity it is you haven't been brought up better! No – I don't want you to be nosey. You can be cheeky. Yes – you can be CHEEKY – CHEEKY – CHEEKY!'

And as he spoke, he vanished in a most peculiar way, just as smoke grows thinner and vanishes. Timmy could just hear his voice saying 'CHEEKY' over and over again, and then it stopped, and there was nobody there.

'A dream!' thought Timothy. 'A silly dream. But wasn't I smart in it? My word, I do feel sharp when I'm cheeky.'

He fell asleep. When he got up the next morning, he dressed as usual, and then went to the mirror to brush his hair, and get his parting straight.

He stared at himself in surprise. His cheeks were both very swollen and he looked most peculiar.

'Now what's happened to me?' thought Timmy, half-frightened. He went downstairs and his father and mother gazed at him in dismay.

'Timmy! Have you got toothache, dear? You poor boy, you must go to the dentist,' said his mother.

'I don't want to,' said Timothy. 'I haven't got toothache.'

'You *must* go, Timmy,' said his mother.

'Shan't,' said Timmy, rudely. His father was just going to scold him when he saw that Timmy's left cheek was getting almost like a balloon!

'You're face is getting worse, my boy,' he said. 'Mother, you must take him to the dentist at once.'

So Timmy had to go. The dentist was astonished to see how swollen the boy's cheeks were, and he had a look at his teeth at once. He took a very long time

and Timmy grew impatient.

'Are you going to be all day?' he said. 'It's Saturday and I want to play with Harry.'

The dentist took no notice of Timothy's rudeness. He spoke to his mother. 'I must take a tooth out at the back,' he said. 'It's the only one that I can see that may be causing this terrible swelling.'

So Timothy had a tooth out, but his cheeks didn't go down. No – they seemed even bigger than ever when he left the dentist. His mother looked at him, very worried.

'I wonder if you've got mumps,' she said. 'You know, sometimes your face swells up very much with that. It may be mumps.'

'Mother, I want to go and play with Harry,' said Timmy. 'You make such a fuss! Look – here's Harry's house. I shall go in and play with him. I won't go to the doctor.'

The cheeky, disobedient boy walked in at Harry's gate and knocked at the

door – but as soon as Harry's mother opened it, she cried out in horror to see Timothy's swollen face.

'Go away!' she cried. 'There's something the matter with you. Goodness knows what it is – mumps, perhaps. It may be catching, and I don't want you near Harry. You stay away from school till you are better!'

Timmy's mother heard her. She hurried Timmy away at once to the doctor and he examined the little boy very carefully.

'Very strange,' he said. 'It *may* be mumps, and it may be because of the tooth the dentist took out. Keep him away from all other children till the swelling goes down.'

'I'm going to a party this afternoon,'

said Timmy, at once. 'I don't care what you say!'

The doctor stared at the cheeky little boy and saw that his cheeks were swelling even more. They looked more like balloons than cheeks! He shook his head.

'You'll do as you're told,' he said. 'I'll make you up some medicine to take, which will, I'm afraid, be very nasty. And I'll give you some lotion to bathe your cheeks with. It will smart, but that can't be helped.'

So there was poor Timmy, put to bed on the day of a party, drinking horrible medicine and having his cheeks bathed with a lotion that smarted like stinging-nettles. He felt very sorry indeed for himself and he cried when he was alone. All that day he lay there, seeing nobody, hearing the children go to the party next door. He took his nasty medicine every hour, and had his cheeks bathed every two hours. He looked at himself in the glass, and was filled with horror when he saw how ugly he looked.

'Mother, will I always look as ugly as this?' asked poor Timmy.

'You'll look all right as soon as your cheeks go down,' said his mother, looking worried and anxious. 'Now, see if you can go to sleep for a bit.'

But Timmy couldn't. He lay and listened to the shouts of laughter from next door, and he heard the popping of crackers. Then, after two or three hours, he heard the children going home. And suddenly he got a fright!

Someone was looking in at his

window! It was Harry! He had been to the party next door, and had suddenly thought he would like to have a word with poor Timmy. He had climbed up the old apple tree outside the boy's bedroom, and there he was, grinning through the window.

'Hallo,' said Timmy, hardly able to speak now because his cheeks were so big.

'Timmy! What's the matter with you!' cried Harry, and the grin faded from his face. 'You look simply terrible. I've never seen anyone so ugly in my life.'

'It's awful,' said Timmy. 'I don't know what happened to make me like this. I'm all cheeks.'

'Well,' said Harry, his grin coming back again, suddenly. 'Well – we always knew you were a cheeky boy – and now you certainly are the most CHEEKY person I've ever seen – yes, all cheeks. Perhaps it's because you always were cheeky that you've gone like that!'

A voice called out sternly from below the window. 'Harry! Come down at once. You know you've got your best suit on.'

Harry disappeared suddenly. He didn't dare to be cheeky to *his* mother. He respected her too much. Timmy was left alone, thinking hard.

He remembered the funny dream he had had the night before – when he thought he had seen a brownie. Perhaps it *wasn't* a dream! Perhaps it had been real. Perhaps – perhaps – that little fellow had put a sort of spell on him. Timmy remembered his voice, saying: 'You can be CHEEKY – CHEEKY – CHEEKY!'

'He'll come again tonight to see what has happened,' thought Timothy. 'I'll ask him to make me right again. I can't go on like this – everyone thinking I'm ill, and not coming near me.'

But the brownie didn't come! Timothy never saw him again. So the next day his cheeks were still swollen and he still had to take the medicine and have his face bathed.

He had a lot of time to think. He

began to notice that every time he was rude or cheeky, his cheeks swelled up a little more – but if he answered politely and kindly, they seemed to go down.

'I suppose that the only person who can cure me is myself,' thought Timothy, at last. 'Well, I shall miss school and games and miss going to the circus and going out to tea if I don't do something about it. I shall have to stop being cheeky. It's a pity because it made me feel smart. But I can't have cheek going to my cheeks!'

He began to be polite in his answers. He didn't contradict. He didn't answer back. He didn't interrupt others, and bit by bit his balloon-like cheeks went down, until one day he looked quite himself again. The doctor came to see him and smiled.

'Ah – he's all right again now. He can go back to school. A most peculiar illness. I can't think what it was, even now!'

'It seems to have done him good, doctor,' said Timmy's mother. 'He's so

quiet and polite now – quite a different boy. Not at all cheeky.'

The doctor laughed. 'You're right – he's certainly not CHEEKY any more. Let's hope he won't be either.'

Well, the last time I saw Timothy, he had one cheek just a little bit swollen, but he was hoping nobody would notice. It was harder to get out of the habit of being cheeky than he had thought! Poor Timothy. He had a dreadful time, didn't he, but if it taught him to be polite and well-mannered, it was worth it.

11

Pink Paint for a Pixie

Once, when Linda was playing at the bottom of her garden, she heard a funny noise. She stopped and listened.

'If a bird could speak, it would speak just like that funny voice,' thought Linda, in surprise. 'It *is* somebody talking – it's a very small voice, high and clear.'

She sat perfectly still, listening, trying to hear what the voice said.

'Just my luck!' said the voice. 'Finished the tea-set all but three cups – and now I've run out of paint. Isn't that just my luck?'

Linda quietly popped her head through a gap in the hedge to see who could be talking. It didn't at all sound like a child. It wasn't a child, either.

'It's a pixie!' said Linda, in the greatest surprise. 'Well, who would have thought I'd ever see a pixie! I've looked for years and years and never seen one. But this *must* be one – and he's talking to himself. What is he doing?'

She looked closely and saw that he was painting a very small tea-set, just big enough for himself to drink from. The cups and saucers were about the size of the ones in Linda's doll's house.

Suddenly the tiny fellow heard Linda breathing and he looked up. He stared in surprise at the little girl's head peeping through the hedge.

'Hallo!' he said. 'Isn't it a nuisance – I've run out of pink paint.'

'What are you doing?' asked Linda.

'I'm painting a pretty pattern on these cups,' said the pixie, and he held one up for Linda to see.

He certainly was putting a very pretty pattern on each one. There were pink roses and green leaves all the way around. The saucers and plates had the same pattern.

Linda looked at the tiny tubes of paint beside the pixie. The tube of pink paint was squeezed quite empty.

'Can't you finish your work?' she asked.

'No,' said the pixie. 'And I promised the Princess Peronel she should have the whole set tomorrow, for her birthday party. It's really annoying.'

Linda suddenly had a splendid idea. *She* had some tubes of paint in her paint box. One might be pink. If so, she could lend it to the pixie!

'I believe I could help you,' she said. 'I've got some paints. I'll go and get the tube of pink. Wait here a minute.'

She ran indoors and found her paint box. 'Darling, surely you are not going to paint indoors this fine morning!' said her mother, when she saw Linda getting out her paint-box.

'No, Mummy – I'm lending a tube of pink paint to a pixie,' said Linda.

Her mother laughed. 'What funny things you do say, Linda!' she said. She didn't guess for a minute that Linda

135

was speaking the truth. She thought she was just pretending.

Linda ran out again, holding in her hand a tube of crimson paint. She knew that if the pixie mixed the deep red with water, the colour would be pink. She was soon back at the hedge again.

'Here you are,' she said. 'I'm sure this will make a lovely pink.'

'You *are* a good friend!' said the pixie, gratefully. 'You can watch me paint if you like.'

Linda sat and watched him. He had a tiny china palette on which he mixed his colours. He squeezed some of the crimson out on to it, and then dipped his tiny brush into a dewdrop hanging on a grass nearby. Soon he had just the right pink for the little cups. It was fun to watch him painting roses round the cup he was holding.

'I don't know what I should have done if you hadn't helped me,' he said. 'Can I do anything for you in return?'

'I suppose you couldn't make a wish come true, could you?' asked Linda, at

Pink Paint for a Pixie

once. The pixie shook his head.

'No,' he said. 'I don't know powerful enough magic for that. If I did I'd have wished for a new tube of pink paint for myself. But if you really want a wish to come true why don't you find a four-leaved clover, put it under your pillow, and wish before you go to sleep?'

'There aren't any four-leaved clovers round about here,' said Linda. 'I and the other children have looked and looked, but we have never found one.'

'Well, go to where the foxgloves grow, pick up a fallen foxglove bell, slip it on your thumb and wish,' said the pixie.

'The foxgloves aren't out yet,' said Linda.

'Of course they aren't!' said the pixie. 'How silly of me. Well, try the pink-tipped daisy spell, then.'

'What's that?' asked Linda.

'You pick thirteen pink-tipped daisies,' said the pixie. 'You make them into a daisy-chain, and wear them round your neck for one hour, at four o'clock in the daytime. You wish your wish thirteen times in that hour. Then you take off the chain and put the daisies in water. You mustn't forget to do that, because if you don't give them a drink, the magic won't work.'

'That sounds a good spell,' said Linda. 'But there aren't any pink-tipped daisies round here, pixie. Look – they are quite white.'

The little girl picked two or three daisies and showed them to the pixie. He looked underneath the petals at the very tips. He shook his head.

139

'You're right,' he said. 'Not a pink tip to be seen. Very tiresome. Well, I must think of something else for you.'

A bell rang in the distance. Linda got up. 'That's for my dinner,' she said. 'I must go. I'll come back again afterwards.'

'I'll think of something whilst you are gone,' said the pixie. He thought and he thought. But he could think of no other way of making a wish come true. He was only a small pixie, not very old, and he really didn't know a great deal of magic.

Then a fine idea came into his small head. Hadn't he got plenty of pink paint in that tube? Well, why shouldn't he paint all the daisies round about with pink tips?

'Good idea!' he said, and as soon as he finished his tea-set, he went to the daisies, sat underneath the little flowers, and carefully ran his brush, full of pink paint, under the tip of each petal. Soon the first daisy looked really pretty. It turned up its petals a little to show the

pink underneath.

'I hope Linda comes back soon,' thought the pixie. 'Then I can tell her what I've done.'

But Linda didn't come back. Her mother had said she must have a rest after dinner, and the little girl was on her bed, hoping that the pixie would still be in the field when she got up at three o'clock.

He wasn't. He had packed up his painted tea-set for the Princess Peronel and had gone. But there were the daisies, all pink-tipped! And there was the little tube of paint left beside them, half-empty now, with the top put neatly on.

Linda looked round for the pixie, when she crept out through the hedge into the field after her rest. He wasn't there. But there was her tube of paint – and, oh, what a surprise, it was lying by a daisy-plant, where four pink-tipped daisies grew together, their golden eyes looking straight at Linda!

'He's painted your tips pink! The underneath of your pretty white petal is crimson pink! Now I can try that magic spell!'

Linda picked thirteen daisies and made them into a chain. You know how she made it, don't you? She slit each stalk near its end with a pin, and then slipped a daisy through the slit, so that soon the thirteen were hanging in a pretty chain. She joined the chain – and looked at her watch.

'Four o'clock! Now I'll wear it – and for one hour I will wish my wish thirteen times!'

She wore the daisy-chain, and wished her wish thirteen times in the hour. Then she took off the chain and put the daisies into water to have a drink. She wished for her big soldier-brother to come back from far away – and, will you believe it, he came home the very next day. She rushed out to tell the pixie, but she has never seen him again.

Have you seen pink-tipped daisies? Go out and look for some; maybe you will find thirteen!

Pink Paint for a Pixie

12

Peter's Birthday

Peter woke up on his birthday and saw the sun shining brightly in at his window. He sat up joyfully.

'Proper birthday weather. I'm nine to-day – and Dad always promised me a bicycle when I was nine. I do wonder if he has remembered.'

He dressed and went downstairs – and the very first thing he saw, glittering and shining outside on the verandah, was a brand new bicycle! Peter rushed to it in delight, shouting at the top of his voice.

'Dad, you remembered! Oh, what a beauty!'

'Happy birthday, Peter,' said his father and mother, both together. Then his father stopped him from getting on

his bicycle to ride round the garden.

'Now wait a moment. Before you even get on that bicycle, you've got to read every bit of what the Highway Code says about bicyclists! Every word – and you've got to remember it too!'

Peter looked sulky. 'Oh blow! What's the sense of that? I've learnt to ride already, and I know all about the traffic lights, and putting my hand out to go round corners and things like that.'

'And before you go for your first ride *I* want to say a few things,' said his mother. 'You're so hasty and careless, Peter, and I want to be quite sure you know everything you ought to know before you go riding.'

'Oh, Mother – don't lecture me on my birthday,' groaned Peter. 'It's going to be such a nice day with cards and presents – and my party this afternoon, with a birthday cake and ices! Balloons and crackers! Smashing!'

His mother laughed. 'I'm not lecturing you, you silly boy. It's a mother's duty to tell her children the rules of the

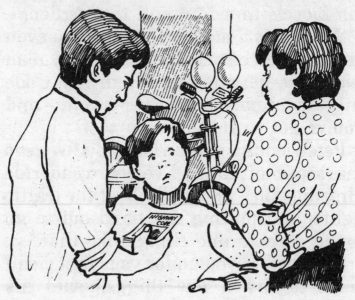

road when they first have a bicycle. Well, I'll tell you after breakfast. Come along now, and see your cards and other presents. You can read the Highway Code before you go out.'

Well, after breakfast the telephone bell rang and his mother went to answer it. His father was going round the garden with the gardener. Peter stood impatiently in the hall, wishing he could go for his first ride.

'I'll just get on my bike and ride down the road and back,' he thought, getting tired of waiting. 'I can't possibly come to any harm! I've ridden round Ned's garden hundreds of times, and I shall be quite safe on the road.'

So he jumped on his bicycle, rode round the garden path, and out of the gate, feeling very happy. His own bright, shining bike! It was wonderful. He rang the bell loudly to tell a dog to get out of the way. He put his hand out to show everyone he was about to go round the corner. He stopped at the traffic lights because they showed red.

It was fun to be out on the road with motors and lorries all about. Better than riding round and round a garden! Peter began pedalling up the steep hill outside the town. He puffed and panted, and then he saw, just in front of him, a lorry going steadily up the hill. Peter pedalled hard to catch it up and then caught hold of the back of the lorry. 'You can jolly well pull me up the hill!' he said to the lorry, and up he went behind it, not pedalling at all.

The lorry got to the top and came to

the level again. Peter still held on, enjoying being towed along. And then things happened all at once, as accidents always do!

A dog ran in front of the lorry. The driver pulled up with a jerk. Peter's bicycle ran straight into the back of the lorry, and he fell off. A car behind didn't pull up in time and ran into the back of the lorry too. Poor Peter and his bicycle were between the car and the lorry.

What a to-do there was! The dog barked. The lorry-driver got down at

once. The driver of the car leapt out. Peter was pulled out of the mess, with bits of broken bicycle sticking to him!

'Why, it's little Peter Brown!' said a woman. 'I'll go and telephone to his mother! Dear, dear – what a silly boy to hang on to the back of a lorry like that. I'm surprised his father and mother didn't tell him the rules of the road!'

Poor Peter! His leg was broken and he had to spend his birthday in hospital.

His bicycle was smashed to bits – his lovely new bicycle! He couldn't eat any birthday cake or pull any crackers.

'It's a dreadful price to pay for a minute's foolishness,' said his father, 'and a terrible way to learn to be careful!'

So it was. I'd rather read the Highway Code and listen to a bit of sound advice, than learn by smashing up my bicycle and my leg, wouldn't you?

13

The Man Who Wasn't Father Christmas

There was once an old man with a long white beard who loved children. He was very poor, so he couldn't give the children anything, and you can guess that he always wished at Christmas-time that he was Father Christmas.

'Goodness! What fun I'd have if I were Father Christmas!' he thought. 'Think of having a sack that was always full of toys that couldn't be emptied, because it was magic. How happy I should be!'

Now one Christmas-time the old man saw a little notice in the window of a big shop. This is what it said:

'WANTED. A man with a white beard to be Father Christmas, and give out paper leaflets in the street.'

Well, the old man stared at this notice,

and wondered if he could get the job. How lovely to dress up as Father Christmas, and go up and down the streets with all the children staring at him! He would be so happy.

So he marched into the shop and asked if he could have the job.

'The work is not hard,' said the shopman. 'All you have to do is to dress up in a red cloak and trousers and big boots, and take a sack with you.'

'Will it be full of toys?' asked the old man, his eyes shining at the thought.

WANTED!
A man with a white beard to be FATHER CHRISTMAS, and give out paper leaflets in the street.

'Of course not!' said the shopman. 'It will be full of leaflets for you to give to the passers-by. I have had these leaflets printed to tell everyone to come to our shop this Christmas and buy their presents here. I thought it would be a good idea to dress somebody up as Father Christmas, and let him give out the leaflets.'

'I see,' said the old man. 'I rather thought it would be nice to give the children something.'

'Well, what an idea!' said the shopman. 'Now, see if this red Father Christmas costume fits you.'

It fitted the old man well. He got into it and looked at himself in the glass. He really looked exactly like old Father Christmas. His long white beard flowed down over his chest and his bright blue eyes twinkled brightly.

He took his sack of leaflets and went out. It was the day before Christmas and everyone was busy shopping. How the children stared when they saw the old man walking along in the road!

'It's Father Christmas!' they shouted. 'It's Father Christmas! Come and see him!'

Soon the children were crowding round the old man, asking if they could peep into his sack. But alas, there were no toys there, and all he had to give the children were the leaflets. The children were disappointed.

'Fancy Father Christmas only giving us leaflets about Mr. White's shop,' they said. 'We thought he was a kind old man – but he isn't. He didn't even give us a sweet.'

The old man heard the children saying these things and he was sad. 'I made a mistake in taking this job,' he said to himself. 'It is horrid to pretend to be somebody kind and not be able to give the boys and girls even a penny! I feel dreadful!'

It began to snow. The old man plodded along the streets, giving out his leaflets. And suddenly he heard a curious sound. It was the sound of bells!

'Where are those bells, I wonder?' thought the old man, looking all round. 'It sounds like horse-bells. But everyone has cars nowadays. There are no horses in this town.'

It wasn't horse-bells he heard. It was reindeer-bells! To the great surprise of the old man, a large sleigh drove down the road, drawn by reindeer. And in it was – well, you can guess without being told – the *real* Father Christmas!

The sleigh drew up, and Father Christmas leaned out. 'Am I anywhere near the town of Up-and-Down?' he called. Then he stared hard at the old man

The Man Who Wasn't Father Christmas

– and he frowned.

'You look like *me!*' he said. 'Why are you dressed like that?'

'Well, just to get a job of work,' said the old man. 'But really because I love children, and I thought if I dressed up like you, they would think I *was* you, and would come round me and be happy. But all I have in my sack is stupid leaflets about somebody's shop – I haven't any toys to give away, as you have. So instead of making the children happy I have disappointed them. I am sorry now I ever took this job.'

'Well, well, you did it for the best,' said Father Christmas, smiling suddenly. 'I like people who love children. They are always the nicest people, you know. Look here – would you like to do me a good turn?'

'I'd love to,' said the old man.

'Well,' said Father Christmas, 'I haven't had any tea, and I feel so hungry and thirsty. Would you mind taking care of my reindeer for me whilst I'm in a tea-shop? They don't like

standing still, so you'll have to drive them round and round the town. And if you meet any children, you must do exactly as I always do.'

'What's that?' asked the old man, his eyes shining.

'You must stop, and say to them, 'A happy Christmas to you! What would you like out of my sack?' And you must let the child dip its hand into my sack and take out what it wants. You won't mind doing that, will you? I always do that as I drive along.'

'*Mind* doing that! It would be the thing I would like best in the world,' said the old man, hardly believing his ears. 'It's – it's – it's – well, I just can't tell you how happy it will make me. I can't believe it's true!'

Father Christmas smiled his wide smile. He jumped down from the sleigh and threw the reins to the old man.

'Come back in an hour,' he said. 'I'll have finished my tea by then.'

He went into a tea-shop. The old man climbed into the driving-seat. He was trembling with joy. He looked at the enormous sack beside him on the seat. It was simply bursting with toys! He cracked the whip and the reindeer set off with a jingling of bells.

Soon they met three children. How those children stared! Then they went quite mad with delight and yelled to the old man: 'Father Christmas! Father Christmas! Stop a minute, do!'

The old man stopped the reindeer. He beamed at the children. 'A happy Christmas to you!' he said. 'What would you like out of my sack?'

'An engine, please,' said the boy.

'A doll, please,' said one of the girls.

'A book, please,' said another girl.

'Dip into my sack and find what you want,' said the old man. And with shining faces the three children dipped in their hands ... and each of them pulled out exactly what he wanted! They rushed home with shouts of joy.

Well, the old man stopped at every child he met, wished them a happy Christmas, and asked them what they

wanted. And dozens of happy children dipped into the enormous sack and pulled out just what they longed for.

At the end of an hour the old man drove the reindeer back to the tea-shop. Father Christmas was waiting, putting on his big fur gloves. He smiled when he saw the bright face of the old man.

'You've had a good time, I can see,' he said. 'Thanks so much. I don't give presents to grown-ups usually – but you might hang up your stocking just for fun tonight. Good-bye!'

He drove off with a ringing of sleigh-bells. The old man went back to the shop in a happy dream, took off his red clothes and went home.

'I've never been so happy before,' he said as he got into bed. 'Never! If only people knew how wonderful it is to give happiness to others! How lucky Father Christmas is to go about the world giving presents to all the boys and girls!'

The old man hung up his stocking, though he felt rather ashamed of it. And when he woke up in the morning, what do you think was in it?

A magic purse was in it – a purse that was always full of pennies! No matter how many were taken out, there were always some left.

'A penny-purse – a magic penny-purse!' cried the old man joyfully. 'My word – what fun I'll have with the children now!'

He does – for he always has a penny to give each one. I wonder if you've ever seen the little penny-purse. It is black and has two letters in silver on the front. They are 'F.C.' I expect you can guess what they stand for!

14

The Blackberry Gnome

Donald and Bess were out blackberrying. They had a basket each, but they couldn't seem to find many berries to put into them.

'They are either unripe, or too squashy,' said Bess. 'We shall never get our basket filled at this rate.'

'We'd better go deeper into the wood,' said Donald. 'I expect most of the best ones have been picked just here.'

So they took a little path that led into the heart of the wood. They thought it was a proper path, but it wasn't. It was a rabbit path, very narrow and winding. It led the two children into a shady part of the wood, where the sunshine trickled through here and there, and lay in little pools on the bushes and grass.

'Listen!' said Bess, suddenly stopping short. 'Can you hear something?'

Donald listened. He heard a thin clear whistling noise coming from not far away.

'Is it a bird?' he whispered to Bess. 'I've never heard a bird that whistled quite like that before. I do wonder what kind it is.'

Both children were fond of birds, so they crept quietly forward to find out what sort it was that was singing such a sweet little song. They went down on their hands and knees, and crawled silently through the bushes, getting nearer and nearer to the whistler.

But it wasn't a bird after all! The children could hardly believe their eyes. It was the funniest little man they had ever seen. He had a little brown face with bright bird-like eyes, and pointed ears that stuck out on each side. He was dressed in a yellow tunic, bright blue knickerbockers, and long green stockings. His hat had a blue feather in it. He wasn't even as tall as Bess.

'What is he? A brownie?' whispered Bess.

'No, a gnome, I should think,' answered Donald. 'Sh! Don't let him see us. Watch what he is doing.'

The little man was working hard, whistling his thin sweet tune all the time. He had a big pile of baskets on the ground beside him, and he was picking blackberries from the bushes and filling the baskets at a great rate.

Bess and Donald had never seen anyone pick blackberries so fast. They could hardly see his hands, so quickly did they move. Basket after basket was filled, and set neatly down in the shade. At last, when the last one was full, the gnome paused and wiped his hot forehead with an enormous yellow handkerchief.

'That's done!' he said. 'Now I really must go and get a drink. I'm so thirsty.'

The children watched him go to an old oaktree nearby. He took a key from his belt, put it into the trunk, turned it, and hey presto! A little door opened into the tree!

Bess and Donald started in astonishment. What an adventure this was! The gnome disappeared into the tree, and the children heard the sound of something being poured out of a jug.

Then something strange happened. The bush just opposite the children was parted in the middle, and two or three mischievous little faces looked out.

'Come on,' said the owner of one of the faces. 'He's in his tree. It's safe for a moment!'

Out of the bush scampered about twenty tiny creatures, rather like pixies, but with little wings on their ankles and wrists instead of on their backs. Their feet made a pit-a-pat noise as they ran, like drops of rain on the ground.

Before the children could say a word the naughty little creatures had each picked up a basket of blackberries and run off with it! Bess and Donald looked at one another.

'Well!' said Donald. 'The bad little things! Whatever will that gnome say when he finds his lovely blackberries

The Blackberry Gnome

gone?'

'We'd better tell him when he comes back,' said Bess.

'Sh! Here he comes!' said Donald.

The gnome jumped out from his tree, shut the door and locked it. Then he ran whistling to where he had left his baskets of fruit. When he saw there was none there, he stopped his whistling in dismay.

'Wh-wh-wh-what!' he cried. 'Wh-wh-wh-where have my blackberries gone? Oh dear. Oh dear! OH DEAR!'

He looked so funny, that Bess and Donald, although they were sorry for him, couldn't help laughing. He heard them and came rushing round the bush behind which they sat.

'You wicked robbers!' he cried. 'You bad naughty children! You've stolen my blackberries, and now you're laughing at me!'

Bess and Donald stopped smiling at once.

'Of course we haven't taken your blackberries!' began Donald. But the

little man wouldn't take any notice of him, and stormed furiously. Then he clapped his hands loudly.

Through the trees came running half a dozen little men just like the blackberry gnome. They ran up to him, and asked what was the matter.

'These wicked children have stolen all the blackberries that I have been growing for the Fairy Queen's party, and only picked this morning!' cried the gnome. 'Take them away at once and lock them up!'

The gnomes took hold of Bess and Donald, and although they struggled hard, they could do nothing against the determined little men.

'Leave us alone!' cried Donald. 'I tell you we didn't take the blackberries. It was –'

'Be quiet,' said the blackberry gnome fiercely. 'What were you hiding for then? Of course you took the blackberries.'

'We didn't,' said Bess, beginning to cry. 'It was the –'

But it was no use. The gnomes wouldn't listen to a word. They dragged the two children to a big oak tree not very far away, and opened a door in the side. They bundled them in, locked the door, set one of their number on guard, and went off.

It was dark in the oak tree, but little by little the children made out a tiny room, with a little bed in one corner, and a table in another. There were two chairs, much too small for them to sit on, so they sat on the floor.

'It's a shame!' said Donald, trying to comfort poor Bess. 'Nasty little man! Why didn't he listen to what we had to say?'

Bess wouldn't be comforted. She wept loudly. Suddenly an anxious little voice came down from above.

'Who is that crying?'

Donald peered up. Far above he could see the daylight, for the hole in the tree went a good way up.

'Who are you?' he asked.

'I am Frisky the Squirrel,' said the

voice.

'What, the Frisky who lives in our garden?' cried Donald in delight.

'Yes!' said the voice in surprise. 'Why, you must be Donald and Bess! However did you come to be here?'

Quickly Donald told his story, and the squirrel listened.

'It's a shame – it really is,' said Frisky. 'I shall go straight to the Fairy Queen herself, and tell her all you say.' He disappeared, and for a long time there was silence. Then there came the sound of voices outside the tree. At last the children heard a key put into the door, and it swung open.

'Come out,' said the gruff voice of the gnome on guard.

Bess and Donald climbed out, blinking at the bright daylight. Outside was a carriage of gleaming mother-of-pearl, drawn by two swallow-tail butterflies. In it sat the daintiest little person the children had ever seen. They knew her at once, for they had often seen pictures of her.

'The Fairy Queen!' whispered Donald to Bess. 'Frisky kept his word. He went and told her all about us!'

'Isn't she lovely,' whispered back Bess.

'These are the children I told you of,' said the voice of Frisky the Squirrel, and the children saw that he was on a branch just above the Queen's head.

'Tell me your story,' said the Queen, gently. So Donald told her everything. By this time a little crowd of gnomes and brownies had crept around, the blackberry gnome among them, looking rather foolish.

'Why didn't you listen to the children's story before locking them up?' asked the Fairy Queen, turning to the blackberry gnome.

'Sorry, Your Majesty,' mumbled the gnome. 'But who were these creatures that stole the fruit, if the children didn't? That's what I should like to know!'

'I can't tell you who they were,' said Donald. 'They didn't look quite like any fairy-folk I've ever seen pictures of. But their feet sounded just like drops of rain.'

'The Pit-a-Pats! The Pit-a-Pats! It must have been the Pit-a-Pats!' cried

everyone. 'Oh, the naughty little things!'

'Take me to the cave of the Pit-a-Pats,' commanded the Queen. 'Jump in beside me, children. And you, blackberry gnome, had better come too.'

So off they all went through the wood. Frisky the Squirrel went with them, jumping from tree to tree in front of the carriage. After about fifteen minutes they came to a cave, set deep in the wood. It had a big stone in front instead of a door.

'Open, open!' cried the blackberry gnome. But it did not open. A little voice came from inside the cave.

'Ha, ha! blackberry gnome! Is it you? You have come too late! We have eaten all your blackberries.'

'Open in the name of the Queen!' cried the blackberry gnome, angrily. At once there was a frightened silence. Then the stone swung aside, and out came the same naughty little pit-a-pat creatures that the children had seen before.

They flung themselves down in front of the Queen's carriage, and begged for pardon. But the Queen was angry, and spoke sternly to them, in a cold little voice.

'This is the fourth time this week you have been naughty. I shall send you to Arran the Spider, and he will teach you to work hard, and then you will have no

time to be wicked.'

At this a great spider came up, and threw a silver thread around the little kneeling folk. He led them all off into the wood, and the last that Bess and Donald heard of them was a loud weeping and wailing.

'I'm not sure that you don't need punishing too, blackberry gnome,' said the Queen. 'You had no right to shut these children up without listening to what they had to say.'

'Please forgive him,' begged Bess. 'We don't mind now that everything is all right, and it really was very hard to lose all his lovely blackberries as he did.'

'You're a kind little girl,' said the Queen. 'I must do something to make up to you both for the unkind treatment you have had today. Would you like to come to my party tonight?'

'Ooh!' said Bess. Donald couldn't say a word. This was too good to be true.

The Queen laughed.

'You shall come,' she said. 'Frisky shall show you the way home now, and he will call for you at eleven o'clock tonight. Don't be late!'

Then the Queen told them to get out of her carriage and follow Frisky. They thanked her very much, said good-bye, and then went after the squirrel, who was simply delighted to think that his two friends were to go to the party.

The blackberry gnome ran after them.

'Please forgive me,' he said. He looked so unhappy that Bess hugged him.

'Don't worry,' she said. 'It was worth being locked up in that nasty old tree to get an invitation from the Fairy Queen!'

They ran home – and you can just imagine how excited they were all the rest of the day, waiting and waiting for eleven o'clock to come!

15

Paddy-Paws and the Stars

One night Paddy-Paws the rabbit was looking at the sky when he saw a shooting star. It rushed down the sky, and made a long bright trail. Then it vanished.

Paddy-Paws was astonished. He had never seen such a thing before.

'Whiskers and tails!' he said. 'That was a star falling! The moon will fall next, and then what a to-do there'll be. And oh, my goodness – if that isn't the star under the hedge!'

He looked in fright at something that shone in the hedge. He felt quite certain that it was the fallen star. Dear me, what a surprising thing!

'I must go and tell Velvet-Coat the mole,' said Paddy-Paws. So off he went

185

to where Velvet-Coat was throwing up a big mound of earth.

'I say, Velvet-Coat,' said Paddy-Paws. 'What do you think has happened? Why, a star has fallen from the sky, and it's under the hawthorn hedge at this very moment. I saw it there!'

'Good gracious!' cried Velvet-Coat in astonishment. 'Is it really so? Let's go and tell Prickles the hedgehog.'

So off they went to where Prickles was curled up in a spiky ball.

'I say, Prickles,' said Paddy-Paws, 'what do you think has happened? Why, a star has fallen from the sky and it's under the hawthorn hedge at this very moment. I saw it there!'

'My gracious goodness!' said Prickles, uncurling himself in surprise. 'Is that really so? Let's go and tell Bushy the squirrel!'

So off they went to where Bushy was looking for seeds in a pine cone.

'I say, Bushy,' said Paddy-Paws, 'what do you think has happened? Why, a star has fallen from the sky, and it's

under the hawthorn hedge at this very moment. I saw it there.'

'Oh my, oh my!' said Bushy, dropping the pine cone in his surprise. 'Is that really so? Let's go and tell Sharp-Eyes the fox.'

So off they went to where Sharp-Eyes the Fox was cleaning his fur with his tongue.

'I say, Sharp-Eyes,' said Paddy-Paws, keeping a good distance from the fox. 'What do you think has happened? Why, a star has fallen from the sky, and it's under the hawthorn hedge at this very moment. I saw it there!'

'Tails and whiskers!' said Sharp-Eyes in surprise. 'Is that really so? Let's go and tell Brock the badger.'

So off they went to find Brock, but he was far away on the hillside, and it was some time before he came to his burrow again. He found all the animals sitting outside waiting for him.

'I say, Brock,' said Paddy-Paws, 'what do you think has happened? Why, a star has fallen from the sky, and it's

under the hawthorn hedge at this very moment. I saw it there!'

'What a very surprising thing!' said Brock, most astonished. 'Let us go and see it.'

So Paddy-Paws the rabbit, Velvet-Coat the mole, Prickles the hedgehog, Bushy the squirrel, Sharp-Eyes the fox and Brock the badger all went to see the fallen star under the hawthorn hedge. There it shone, all by itself.

'Look at that!' said the animals, and they sat down at a little distance from it.

'Go and get it,' said Sharp-Eyes to Paddy-Paws.

'I'm afraid,' said Paddy-Paws.

'So am I,' said Velvet-Coat.

'I daren't go near it,' said Prickles.

'Nor dare I,' said Bushy.

'Well, I'm not afraid!' said Brock the badger, and he got up to get the star. And at that very moment it moved! Only a little way, but it moved!

'Ooh! Oooh!' cried all the animals, and they scuttled away as fast as ever they could go. Paddy-Paws went to his burrow, Velvet-Coat vanished underground too, Prickles hid himself in a ditch, Bushy ran up a tree, Sharp-Eyes ran to his lair, and Brock lumbered away to his hillside. None of them wanted to touch the fallen star.

When they had all gone, a little tinkling laugh rang out in the hedge, and a small elf leapt down to the star.

'Oh, how funny!' she cried. 'They're all afraid of you, little glow-worm! They think you're a fallen star! You're not, are you! You're just a dear little glow-

Paddy-Paws and the Stars

worm, shining in the night. I'm not afraid of you!'

She picked it up, and popped it into her lantern to light her way through the dark wood – and next morning when all the animals came to see what the star looked like in the daytime, it was gone!

'Where's it gone to?' said Paddy-Paws.

'Back to the sky!' said Brock the badger. And none of them could think why an elf nearby laughed so loudly at them!